Disney PRINCESS

Beauty and the Beast

Dream of Adventure

PRINCESS4067

PaRragon

Bath · New York · Cologne · Melbourne · Delhi
Hong Kong · Shenzhen · Singapore

A young woman named Belle lives in a sleepy, little town.

Belle dreams of going on great adventures like the ones she reads about in her favorite books.

A beast lives in a castle. He was once a prince, but then an enchantress changed him into a beast to punish him for being selfish.

The enchantress also put a spell on the prince's castle and turned his servants into objects!

To break the spell, the Beast must learn to love before the last petal falls from a magic rose.

Belle's father, Maurice, is a clever inventor.

Belle finds her favorite story in the
town bookshop and settles down to read.

The townspeople think that Belle is strange
because she always has her nose in a book.

A young man named Gaston wants to
marry Belle because she is beautiful.

Belle would prefer to read than spend time with Gaston.

Gaston doesn't share Belle's love of books.
He thinks that reading is a waste of time.

Gaston is determined to make Belle his wife.
He gets his friend LeFou to help him.

Belle sees smoke coming out of her cottage. She rushes home to find her father making a brand-new invention.

Sometimes Maurice's inventions go wrong,
but Belle knows that he will be famous one day.

Soon, Maurice's new invention is ready.
He decides to show it at the town fair.

Belle's father packs up his machine and sets off for the fair with his horse, Philippe.

Belle waves good-bye and wishes her father good luck.

Philippe is frightened by the howling wolves in the forest.
Poor Maurice is thrown to the ground by his horse!

Maurice escapes from the wolves through some tall iron gates.
Then he sees a magnificent castle.

Inside the castle, Maurice picks up a candlestick and discovers that it can talk! It is Lumiere, one of the enchanted servants.

Maurice also meets a clock named Cogsworth.

The servants welcome their new guest.

Maurice drinks tea from a little cup named Chip.

There is even a comfy stool that acts like a puppy dog!

Suddenly, the Beast appears.
He is angry to find a stranger in his castle.

The Beast grabs Maurice and throws him into the dungeon.

Meanwhile, Gaston and LeFou have arranged
a wedding so that Gaston can marry Belle.

The only problem is, Belle has not agreed to marry Gaston yet!

Gaston enters Belle's cottage to propose to her. Then he spies himself in a mirror and can't help admiring his reflection!

Gaston tells Belle how lucky she would be to marry him,
but Belle thinks that he is rude and unkind.

Belle says she can't marry Gaston. Then she throws him out of the cottage, and he tumbles straight into a muddy pond!

Belle daydreams about a more exciting life
far away from Gaston and her little town.

Meanwhile, Maurice is in danger and Belle has no idea.

When Philippe returns to the cottage without her father,
Belle knows that something is wrong.

Philippe brings Belle to the castle, where he last saw Maurice.
Inside, Belle sees the terrifying Beast.

Belle finds her father in the dungeon and offers to take his place.
The Beast agrees, but says that she must stay in the castle forever.

Maurice hurries back to the town and tells everyone about the Beast.
The townspeople laugh at Maurice and don't believe him.

Gaston is angry that Belle refused to marry him.

Back at the castle, Belle is comforted by the kindly servants.

The Beast invites his prisoner to join him for dinner.
When she refuses, he loses his temper.

Mrs. Potts and Chip are delighted
to have a new guest in the castle.

The servants prepare a delicious dinner for Belle
and entertain her with music and singing.

After dinner, Belle wants to explore. Cogsworth and Lumiere try to stop her from entering the forbidden west wing.

Belle slips away from her new friends. She finds herself in a mysterious room and sees a beautiful rose under a glass dome.

Suddenly, a figure comes out of the darkness—it is the Beast!

He rushes to guard the rose and angrily orders Belle to leave.

Belle is frightened. She escapes into the forest with Philippe.
Soon, a pack of hungry wolves appears.

The Beast leaps out from the trees and fights off the wolves!
The wolves run away, and Belle is safe.

But the Beast is hurt. Belle puts him on Philippe's back and takes him home to the castle.

Belle looks after the Beast and thanks him
for saving her life.

In the town, Gaston plots to have Maurice taken away to
Monsieur D'Arque's asylum—unless Belle agrees to marry him.

Meanwhile, Belle begins to enjoy spending time at the castle.

The Beast is happy that his guest is no longer afraid of him.

He shows the beautiful library to Belle
and says that it now belongs to her.

The servants hope that the Beast will
learn to love and break the spell.

In the snowy gardens, Belle shows the Beast how to feed the birds.

Thanks to Belle, the Beast learns how to be gentle and kind.

Even the little birds are no longer afraid of him.

Belle and the Beast are becoming good friends.

The pair reads a story beside the roaring fire.

That evening, the enchanted wardrobe helps Belle get ready
for dinner by giving her a lovely yellow dress to wear.

The Beast needs a little help from the servants to get ready, too!

Finally, it's time for the Beast to greet Belle.

She comes down the stairs in her beautiful gown.

After dinner, Belle teaches the Beast how to dance.

Cogsworth and Lumiere can see that
the two friends are beginning to fall in love.

Belle tells the Beast that she is very happy at the castle, but that she also misses her father.

The Beast shows her his magic mirror, which lets him see anyone.
Belle looks into it and sees that her father is very ill.

The Beast gives the mirror to Belle and says that she is free to leave the castle. Belle rushes home to take care of Maurice.

Belle and her father are so happy to be together again.

Chip sneaks into Belle's bag and comes along with her!

Monsieur D'Arque arrives to take Maurice to the asylum.

Gaston tells Belle that if she agrees to marry
him he will save her father. Belle refuses.

Belle uses the magic mirror to show everyone the Beast.
It proves that her father was telling the truth.

The townspeople are terrified.
Gaston decides to kill the Beast.

Gaston locks Belle and her father in their cellar.
They try to escape, but they can't get out.

Gaston leads a group of people from
the town to the Beast's castle.

The servants are shocked to see the band
of angry townspeople getting closer.

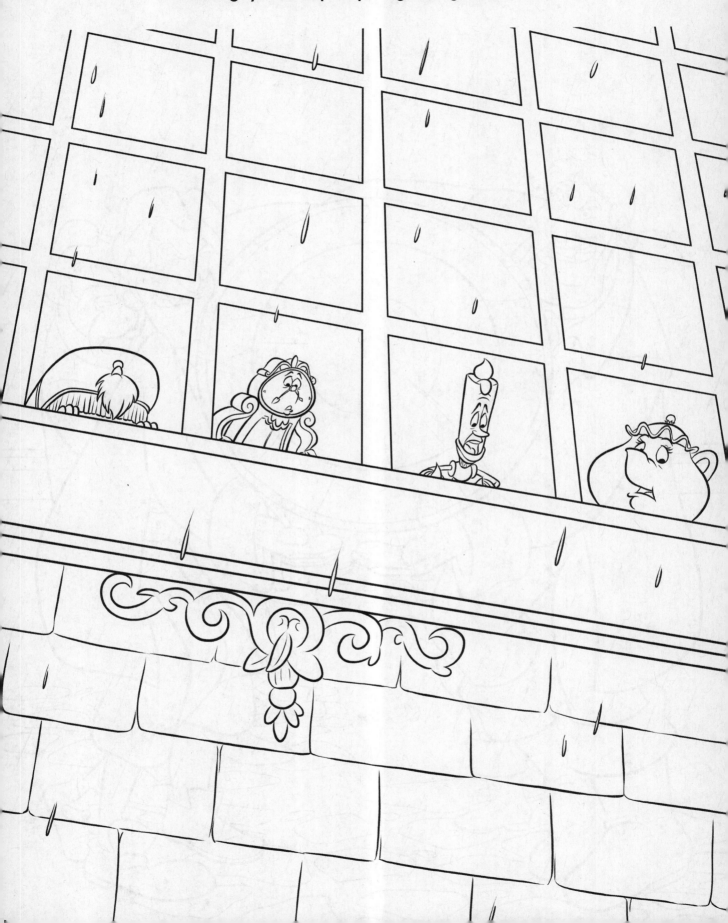

Gaston's mob uses a tree trunk
to break through the castle doors.

Suddenly, the townspeople rush into the castle, and the battle begins!
The brave servants chase the intruders away.

Back in the town, Chip has an idea. He uses Maurice's invention to help Belle and her father escape from their cellar.

Gaston is still inside the castle.
He raises his bow and arrow to attack the Beast.

Without Belle, the Beast loses hope.
He does not try to fight back.

Gaston wounds the Beast,
then raises a club to strike the final blow.

Out of the cellar at last, Maurice and Belle hurry back
to the castle to help the Beast and the servants.

The Beast sees Belle from the tower.
She gives him the hope he needs to defend himself.

Belle knows that the Beast is in danger.
She runs up the stairs to reach him.

The Beast is helped back to safety by Belle,
and Gaston falls from the balcony.

The Beast collapses. Belle tells him that she loves him, just as the last petal falls from the enchanted rose.

The servants think it is too late for the spell to be broken.

Just then, beams of light explode from the Beast, and he begins to transform.

The Beast changes into a handsome prince.

The spell is broken, and the servants are transformed, too!

Little Chip is so happy to be a boy again.

Belle and the prince live happily ever after.